Short Tales
NATIVE AMERICAN MYTHS

THE COLORS OF
A SUNSET

AN ALGONQUIN NATURE MYTH

Adapted by Anita Yasuda
Illustrated by Estudio Haus

magic wagon

visit us at www.abdopublishing.com

Published by Magic Wagon, a division of the ABDO Group, PO Box 398166, Minneapolis, MN 55439. Copyright © 2013 by Abdo Consulting Group, Inc. International copyrights reserved in all countries. All rights reserved. No part of this book may be reproduced in any form without written permission from the publisher.

Short Tales™ is a trademark and logo of Magic Wagon.

Printed in the United States of America, North Mankato, Minnesota.
052012
092012

♻ THIS BOOK CONTAINS AT LEAST 10% RECYCLED MATERIALS.

Adapted text by Anita Yasuda
Illustrations by Estudio Haus
Edited by Rebecca Felix
Series design by Craig Hinton

Design elements: Diana Walters/iStockphoto

Library of Congress Cataloging-in-Publication Data
Yasuda, Anita.
  The colors of a sunset : an Algonquin nature myth / by Anita Yasuda ; illustrated by Estudio Haus.
      p. cm. -- (Short tales Native American myths)
  ISBN 978-1-61641-879-3
 1. Algonquin Indians--Folklore. 2. Algonquin mythology. I. Estudio Haus (Firm) II. Title.
  E99.A349Y37 2012
  971.3004'9733--dc23
                              2012004687

MYTHICAL CHARACTERS

ALGONQUIN CHIEF

The questing hero, young boy's father

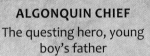

KISISOKWE

The wise medicine woman

PODONCH

An enormous tadpole and lake guardian

SON

A cheerful young boy

MOTHER

Young boy's mother

INTRODUCTION

This legend comes from the Algonquin people. Today, many Algonquin live in Ontario and Quebec in Canada. Algonquin stories often feature the Algonquin's surroundings of forests and lakes. Animals often play important roles in stories because the Algonquin believe that animals once governed the world.

The Colors of a Sunset comes from records written by Juliette Gauthier de La Verendrye. La Verendrye studied the Algonquin. She learned that the sun was honored at sunrise and sunset with dance and music in Algonquin villages.

The lake in *The Colors of a Sunset* is believed to be Lac Nominingue, which is located about 100 miles (161 km) northwest of Montreal in Canada. The legend does not name the lake, but it describes the brightly colored red clay of Lac Nominingue.

Long, long ago, a baby boy was born to an Algonquin chief and his wife. They were very proud of him.

The boy was a cheerful child. He made everyone happy.

But each evening, the boy's family felt sad. When the shadows grew long and the sun sank lower in the sky, the young boy would begin to cry.

The boy's parents tried everything to stop their child from crying. But nothing soothed him. As his Algonquin village became bathed in the colors of the sunset, the boy would cry and cry.

Finally, the boy's parents decided to gather their tribe and ask them for help. Among the tribe members they called together was a medicine woman.

The medicine woman's name, Kisisokwe, meant Sun Woman. She was very wise and deeply respected.

The boy's parents told Kisisokwe about their son.

"As the sky fills with brilliant hues of orange and red, our son cries," they said. "He can't be comforted. Please help us."

Kisisokwe knew what the problem was. She told the parents, "Your child is sad because he wants the colors of the sunset more than anything else."

The chief and his wife were surprised. They loved their son deeply and wanted to give him everything.

"How can we give the sun's special colors to our son?" they wondered.

The colors of the sunset were not something that people could hope to possess. They turned again to Kisisokwe.

The medicine woman had the answer. Kisisokwe told the boy's parents of a special lake that held these colors. It was far from their home.

"At the bottom of this lake," explained wise Kisisokwe, "you will find the colors of the sunset."

The chief would do anything to make his son happy. He set out on a quest for the colors the very next day.

The chief left the village by canoe. He paddled and paddled for many days. At last, he came upon the lake Kisisokwe had spoken of.

The lake was guarded by many strange creatures. The chief was very surprised. He had never seen anything like them before.

One of the guardians of the lake was an enormous tadpole. His name was Podonch. He had a large belly and a tiny mouth.

The chief knew that Podonch would never let him enter the lake. But he didn't want to return to his son without the colors. He would have to sneak past Podonch.

The chief quietly crept up on the giant tadpole. Before Podonch could call for help, the chief grabbed him.

Quickly, the chief used glue from a sturgeon fish to seal Podonch's mouth. Now Podonch could not warn the other animals.

With a mighty shove, the chief pushed Podonch into the water.

The chief dove into the lake. He swam deeper and deeper looking for the colors of the setting sun. At last, he reached the bottom of the lake.

The chief searched the bottom of the lake and found the colors. He gathered them and swam up, up, up to the lake's surface. How pleased his son would be!

The chief quickly set off for his village.
When he reached home, his arrival was
greeted with joy.

At twilight that evening and each one after, the chief gave his son the colors from the lake to play with. From that day forward the boy did not cry, even when the shadows grew long in the village.

But what happened to Podonch? When the other animals discovered Podonch had failed to guard the lake, they were very angry.

"How could you have allowed the chief to take the secret colors of the sun, Podonch?" they cried.

The animals came to a decision. "We will punish you for not guarding our lake, Podonch," they said.

The animals ruled that Podonch was to only breathe through gills. And this is how he stayed.

Since that time, tadpoles have been born with gills and small, puckered-up mouths. This is a reminder to all animals and people that Podonch let the colors of the sunset be stolen. As for the Algonquin village, it is forever bathed in red and orange.